For my brother Paul, who gives to the poor;
Jo, the middle daughter; and of course, the incomparable Jamal
L. A. S.

Pour le dupster, Tifenn
M. G.

Text copyright © 2007 by Laura Amy Schlitz
Illustrations copyright © 2007 by Max Grafe

First edition 2007

Library of Congress Cataloging-in-Publication Data is available.

Library of Congress Catalog Card Number pending

ISBN 978-0-7636-2730-0

2 4 6 8 10 9 7 5 3 1

Printed in China

This book was typeset in Golden Cockerell Roman.
The illustrations were done in mixed media on paper.

Candlewick Press
2067 Massachusetts Avenue
Cambridge, Massachusetts 02140

visit us at www.candlewick.com

The BEARSKINNER

A TALE OF THE BROTHERS GRIMM

retold by **Laura Amy Schlitz**

illustrated by **Max Grafe**

CANDLEWICK PRESS
CAMBRIDGE, MASSACHUSETTS

They say that when a man gives up hope,

the devil walks at his side.

So begins this story:

A soldier marched through a dark wood,

and he did not march alone.

IT WAS WINTER. The soldier's uniform hung in rags; his boots were cracked, and his pockets were empty. *If I had gold,* he thought, *I would go to an inn and order roast duck and a bottle of wine.* But he knew he would go to sleep hungry that night, lying on the hard ground. He was used to that. He had run away to war when he was a boy. Now that the war was over, he had nowhere to go. His childhood home was ashes, and all he loved were dead.

The wind shredded the clouds. All at once, the moon shone, casting a blue light through the trees. The soldier saw the one who had shadowed him: a handsome devil, dressed in a long green coat. His right foot was clad in a black leather boot, but his left foot was the hoof of a goat. That was how the soldier knew who he was.

"What do you want?" demanded the soldier.

"Nothing!" answered the devil. "You're the one who's hungry and cold. You'd sell your soul for a hot supper and a soft bed."

"Never," said the soldier, because he knew that the man who sells his soul becomes the devil's slave and burns in hell.

The devil shrugged. "The choice is yours. I should like to make you rich. But if you are afraid —"

"I fear nothing," said the soldier.

"We shall see," said the devil, and he pointed to the thicket. "Look there!"

The soldier wheeled around. The branches moved; behind them was something strong and dark, with fierce gleaming eyes. If there was anything the soldier knew how to do, it was shoot straight. He raised his rifle and fired.

Down fell the bear with a bullet in its heart.

"Brave fellow!" laughed the devil. "Here is the game I should like to play! For the next seven years, I will see to it that your pockets are full of gold — more than you can ever spend. But during those seven years, you must follow my rules. If you break them, your soul is mine. Otherwise, you will be rich your whole life long — and your soul will remain your own."

"What are the rules?" asked the soldier.

The devil offered him a knife. "First, skin the bear."

The soldier took the knife. It was so sharp that the bear's pelt slid off like the skin of a peach. The devil took the wet bearskin and draped it around the soldier. He leaned so close that the soldier felt the heat of his breath.

"You will be called Bearskinner," the devil said softly. "For seven years, you will wander the world, clad in this skin. Inside it, you will find a pocket that can never be emptied; you will have all the gold you need. But during the seven years, you may not wash or cut your hair or trim your beard or file your nails. And during those years, you may tell no one of the bargain we have struck — and you must not pray to God. If, during the seven years, you kill yourself, your soul is mine."

The soldier stood silent. His fists were clenched.

"Open your hands," said the devil, "and touch what will be yours!"

The soldier groped until he found the pocket in the bearskin. He drew out a handful of treasure: gold and silver and gemstones. It seemed to him that he smelled spiced wine and roasting meat and bread hot from the oven. He swayed on his feet, dizzy with hunger and desire.

"Do you accept the bargain?" asked the devil.

"I do," said the soldier. He left the devil in the wood and marched to the next town, where he had his roast duck and the wine he craved. And that night he slept in a clean white bed.

So began the first year. The soldier bought everything he wanted: food and wine, trinkets and treasures. He was so rich that every door was open to him. He grew filthy, and the bearskin stank, but he bore the stench and the filth bravely.

By the second year, he no longer looked like a man in a bearskin. He looked like a bear, with thick yellow claws and a matted beard. Lice gnawed at his flesh, and he raked himself until he was covered with scabs. People began to mock him.

By the third year, he no longer looked like a bear, but like a monster. The rotting bearskin felt as heavy as iron. Children pelted him with stones. Men and women fled from him. It was only when he brought out his money that they let him come near. Then they bowed before him as if he were a prince. The Bearskinner despised them for their greed. He loathed himself. He began to dream. Night after night, he dreamed that he drowned himself in the river that ran snake-like through the city. The dreams haunted him. He knew that if he ended his life, the devil would gain his soul.

But at last the night came when he left his bed and went to the river. He stood on the bridge and stared through the rain at the black water. He wanted to shriek, "Oh, God!" but he shut his lips, because that was a prayer.

At that moment, he heard the sound of someone crying. The sobs rose up from under his feet. He followed the sound. A woman and her child had taken shelter under the bridge. The night was raw, and the child shivered and wailed. When the woman saw the Bearskinner, she tried to flee. But she was faint from hunger and the child in her arms was heavy. The woman fell to her knees.

The Bearskinner was filled with pity. "Don't be afraid," he said. He reached into the bear's pouch. "Look, here's money. Take it." And because he saw that she was too frightened to approach, he threw the coins, tossing handful after handful of gold onto the wet earth.

The woman stared. Then she crept forward and touched one of the coins.

"That's right!" said the Bearskinner. "Take them all — they're of no use to me! Buy food for the child." He backed up a step, and the woman lifted her head. "God bless you!" she cried.

The Bearskinner's heart leaped. "Pray for me!" he begged. All at once he saw how he might live. He would use the devil's money to feed the poor people of the city.

And so he did. The soldier grew more and more repulsive; his bearskin crawled with maggots, and he reeked. But he no longer hated himself, and he lived in the hope that he would defeat the devil. And the poor of the city blessed him.

Now the soldier's dreams changed. Often he dreamed that he walked in a cloud of butterflies. They shimmered with color, surrounding him so closely that they shielded him from the devil. When he awoke, he knew that the butterflies were the prayers of the poor.

And another year went by.

In the fourth year, the soldier came upon a man who had gambled away his fortune. "I have been a fool," wept the man, "and lost more than I can ever pay. They will put me in prison, and what will become of me?"

"I will pay," said the Bearskinner, and he heaped a great mound of coins in front of the man.

"But what can I do for you?" asked the gambler, and the Bearskinner answered, "Pray for me."

"I will," said the gambler, "but I will do more." He tugged at the soldier's sleeve. "Come home with me. I will give you one of my daughters for a wife. I have three daughters, and all of them are beautiful."

It had been years since anyone invited the soldier home, so he went. The gambler summoned his daughters and told them that one of them must marry the Bearskinner.

The eldest daughter held herself proudly. Her fine eyes flashed. "How dare you, Father?" she asked. "How dare you bring home a creature like that?"

And before her father could answer, the youngest daughter covered her face with her pretty hands. "Oh, Father," she whimpered. "I'm frightened!"

But the middle daughter was neither angry nor afraid. She came and stood before the Bearskinner. She was so close that he caught the fragrance of her hair, and the smell was like apple blossoms. She looked into his eyes as if she were searching for something. The Bearskinner caught his breath.

"I believe you have a good heart," she said. "I will keep my father's word."

The Bearskinner reached into his pouch. From a fistful of trinkets, he drew out a gold ring. He broke it in two. One half he kept. One half he gave to the middle daughter. "Keep this for me," he said. "When I come back, I will ask you to marry me. Wait for me."

And she promised.

The Bearskinner returned to his wanderings. For three more years, he traveled the world, giving away the devil's gold. Often he thought of the gambler's daughter and wondered if she would keep her promise.

At last the seven years were over. The Bearskinner made his way back to the wood where he had first met the devil. It was winter again, and the skull of the slain bear lay on the grass. The devil came slowly, dragging his goat's hoof.

The soldier smiled at the devil. "I have won."

The devil said, "Your soul is your own," as if the words tasted bitter to him.

"Wait!" commanded the soldier. "We are not quite finished with each other. For seven years, you made me dirty. Now you will make me clean."

The soldier made the devil drag the rotted bearskin off his shoulders. He forced the devil to cut his hair and trim his nails and wash him. The devil gnashed his teeth and gagged, but the soldier had mastered him, and the devil had to do his bidding. When at last he was clean, the soldier took the devil's green coat. He wrapped it around his nakedness and walked off barefoot, whistling.

The next day he bought new clothes. He rode to the gambler's house on a dapple-gray horse. As he trotted through the streets, he looked so merry and gallant that people turned their heads to stare after him.

When he knocked at the gambler's door, the gambler did not recognize him. The Bearskinner announced that he was seeking a bride, and the gambler called his daughters. How eager they were to wed this handsome stranger! The oldest daughter fanned him, and the youngest daughter fed him bits of cake as if he were a lap dog. But the middle daughter kept apart, watching him with questioning eyes. At last the soldier asked why she was silent.

"She has promised to marry another," said the eldest daughter. "Such a fierce fellow, too! A great ugly bear of a man!" And the youngest daughter pressed her fingers over her lips and giggled.

"Is that true?" asked the soldier. "Is he really so ugly, this man you are going to marry?"

"His eyes are not ugly," answered the middle daughter. "His eyes are like yours."

The soldier clapped his hands and called for a bottle of champagne. He poured four glasses. He put his half of the gold ring in one goblet and gave it to the middle daughter. When she drank, she glimpsed the bit of shining metal in her wine. Her face lit up, and he held out his hands to her.

"I have come back," said the soldier. "Will you marry me?"

She gave him her hands and said she would. And she looked so happy that her sisters hissed with envy.

So the middle daughter married the Bearskinner. The love between them lasted a lifetime, and so did the soldier's fortune. He always had more than enough, and he always shared with people who had nothing. And never again did he bargain with the devil.